Braulick, Carrie A.
Arabian horses

VALLEY COMMUNITY LIBRARY
739 RIVER STREET
PECKVILLE, PA 18452
(570) 489-1765
www.lclshome.org

ARABIAN HORSES

by Carrie A. Braulick

CAPSTONE PRESS
a capstone imprint

Snap Books are published by Capstone Press,
1710 Roe Crest Drive, North Mankato, Minnesota 56003
www.mycapstone.com

Copyright © 2018 by Capstone Press, a Capstone imprint. All rights reserved. No part of this publication may be reproduced in whole or in part, or stored in a retrieval system, or transmitted in any form or by any means, electronic, mechanical, photocopying, recording, or otherwise, without written permission of the publisher.

Library of Congress Cataloging-in-Publication Data
Names: Braulick, Carrie A., 1975- author. Title: Arabian horses / by Carrie A. Braulick. Description: North Mankato, Minnesota : Capstone Press, [2018] | Series: Snap books. Horse breeds | Audience: Age 8-14. | Includes bibliographical references and index. Identifiers: LCCN 2017038722 (print) | LCCN 2017048698 (ebook) | ISBN 9781543500431 (eBook PDF) | ISBN 9781543500318 (hardcover) | ISBN 9781543500370 (paperback) Subjects: LCSH: Arabian horse--Juvenile literature. | Horse breeds--Juvenile literature. Classification: LCC SF293.A8 (ebook) | LCC SF293.A8 B732 2018 (print) | DDC 636.1/12--dc23 LC record available at https://lccn.loc.gov/2017038722

Editorial Credits
Amy Kortuem, editor
Kayla Rossow, designer
Morgan Walters, media researcher
Kathy McColley, production specialist

Image Credits
Alamy: Hemis, 20; Dreamstime: Janina Kubik, 11; Getty Images: Irfan Khan, 19, MPI, 9; Newscom: Ton Koene/VWPics, 5; Shutterstock: Andrzej Kubik, 1, carlylyn, 4, GeptaYs, 25, halitomer, 15, Irina Mos, (background) spread 2-3, Juliata, (floral)design element throughout, L. Kramer, (fish scale) design throughout, Makarova Viktoria, bottom 13, mariait, top 13, 29, Olga_i, 14, pirita, 23, redstone, (paper background) design element throughout, skmj, 26, suns07butterfly, (watercolor) design element throughout, Tamara Didenko, spread 16-17, Wolfilser, 6, YanLev, 22, yod67, (horse vector) design element, Zuzule, Cover

Printed and bound in the United States.
672

Table of Contents

Chapter 1
A Long History 4

Chapter 2
Not Just a Pretty Face 10

Chapter 3
Champions of Endurance 18

Chapter 4
Arabians in Action 24

Fast Facts: 28

Glossary 30

Read More 31

Internet Sites 31

Index 32

Chapter 1
A Long History

The Bedouin people have lived in the deserts of the Middle East for at least 2,000 years. Early Bedouins formed strong bonds with their horses. They trained the horses to fight in wars. Sometimes they let the horses live with them in their tents. But the Bedouins weren't happy with just any type of horse. They rode only Arabians.

Today's Arabian owners have the same passion for their horses that the Bedouins did. Arabians are one of the world's most popular horse **breeds**.

breed—a group of animals that have the same features and ancestry; breed also means to mate animals so they will produce young

FACT

The Bedouins' Arabians could not eat grass from green pastures. Few plants grew in the desert. The Bedouins sometimes gave their horses dates to eat or camel's milk to drink.

Today people sometimes ride Arabians in outfits based on the Bedouins' clothing.

Early Beginnings

The Arabian is the oldest horse breed. No one knows exactly when the breed began. Ancient Egyptian artwork from around 1300 BC shows horse drawings that look like today's Arabians. The ancient Egyptians may have used Arabians to pull chariots in wars.

Early Bedouins are known for starting the first Arabian breeding programs. They carefully selected the horses they bred. They wanted to produce the best war horses.

Religion and Royalty

By the AD 600s the religion of Islam had gained popularity in the Middle East. Islam's founder, Muhammad, raised Arabians. Mounted on Arabian horses, Muhammad and his followers spread the Islamic faith.

An Arabian Legend

Muhammad's interest in Arabians was so well known that people told many stories about it. One story says that Muhammad once locked up 100 Arabian **mares** to test their courage and loyalty. He didn't give them water for three days. Muhammad then set the thirsty horses free. They ran toward a nearby pool of water. When he called for the horses to return to him, most kept running to the water. But five loyal mares stopped, turned around, and returned to Muhammad. These mares became his favorites. The story says they helped to start the Arabian horse breed.

mare—an adult female horse

The success of Arabians as war horses made them valuable. From the 1200s to the 1800s many Middle Eastern rulers had large Arabian farms. They sent people far into the desert to find the best Arabian horses.

The Breed Spreads

By the late 1800s people in European countries wanted Arabians. In 1881 Wilfred and Anne Blunt brought several Arabian horses from the Middle East to England. They started a large Arabian farm called Crabbet Park. People also started Arabian farms in Germany, Poland, and Hungary.

Arabians also found homes on the other side of the Atlantic Ocean. In 1877 Turkish leaders sent a gift of two Arabian **stallions** to U.S. President Ulysses S. Grant. These horses were part of one of the first U.S. Arabian breeding programs. In 1906 Homer Davenport brought 27 Arabians from the Middle East to the United States.

stallion—an adult male horse that can be used for breeding

registry—an organization that keeps track of the ancestry for horses of a certain breed

THE AHA

American owners of Arabians wanted to keep track of their horses' ancestries. In 1908 the Arabian Horse Club of America formed. Later the **registry** was renamed the Arabian Horse Association (AHA). By 1950 about 5,000 horses were registered with the AHA. Today more than 1 million Arabians are registered with the AHA.

Ulysses S. Grant's Arabian stallion Leopard was the earliest imported Arabian to be registered with the Arabian Horse Club of America.

Chapter 2

Not Just a Pretty Face

Today many horse breeds look different from Arabians. Yet nearly all horses have Arabian **ancestors**. Early horse breeders admired the Arabian's look and skill. They mated Arabians with other types of horses.

Basic Features

Arabians can have gray, bay, chestnut, black, or roan coats. Bay coats are red-brown. All bay horses have black manes and tails. Chestnut coats are a copper color. Roan Arabians have bay, black, or chestnut coats with a mixture of white hair. Like other horses, Arabians may have white leg and face markings.

ancestor—a member of a breed that lived a long time ago

FACT

Arabians are known as a "hot-blooded" breed because of their desert-bred ancestry and their sensitive, spirited personalities.

Arabians have a proud look and a free, long stride.

Horses are measured from the ground to the **withers**. Arabians usually are between 14.2 and 15.2 hands high. A hand equals 4 inches (10 centimeters). Many other breeds are taller. But Arabians can carry a great deal of weight for their size.

A Graceful Horse

Many people think the Arabian is the most beautiful of all horse breeds. It is known for its graceful features. The Arabian has a long, curved neck. Its sloped shoulders are in front of a short, strong back. The Arabian often has a long, full mane and tail. It carries its tail higher than other horses do.

People say the Arabian seems to float as it moves. It steps lightly with long, free strides.

The Arabian's Head

The Arabian's head is one of its most striking features. The small head slopes inward below the eyes. The slope creates a low spot, or dish. The Arabian's large, dark eyes are spaced far apart from each other. Its ears are small and pointed.

withers—the top of a horse's shoulders

The Arabian's head angles down to a small, soft muzzle. Some people say its muzzle looks like it can fit into a teacup.

The dish below the eyes is one of the Arabian's well-known features.

Made to Run

Arabians can run long distances without tiring. They have large nostrils that can take in a great deal of air. For their size Arabians have a deep chest. The chest allows the lungs to enlarge and hold the air brought in through the nostrils.

Arabians also have strong leg bones to help them run long distances. Healthy Arabians that aren't overworked usually have few leg injuries.

Personality

Arabians are more lively and sensitive than most other breeds. Some people think the Arabian's personality makes it hard to train. But Arabians that are handled properly behave well.

The intelligence of Arabians helps them learn quickly. In the late 1970s an Arabian horse named Cass Olé played the starring role in the movie *The Black Stallion*. In only 11 weeks Cass Olé learned to paw, rear, lie down, and perform several other stunts.

Arabians are known to bond well with people. Many horse owners believe Arabians sense people's feelings better than other horses can. Managers of riding programs for people with disabilities often choose Arabians because of these qualities.

Chapter 3
Champions of Endurance

The Arabian's ability to travel long distances without tiring makes it a perfect choice for **endurance** racing. Riders use more Arabians in endurance races than any other breed.

Endurance Races

The American Endurance Ride Conference (AERC) runs most endurance races in the United States and Canada. AERC races are 50 or more miles (80 or more kilometers) long. Beginners sometimes compete in races that 25 to 35 miles (40 to 56 km) long.

endurance—the ability to keep doing an activity for long periods of time

Arabians are the most suitable horses for endurance racing.

FACT

A horse in a 50-mile (80-km) endurance race can lose about 10 gallons (38 liters) of water by sweating.

At checkpoints race workers sometimes cool down the horses with water.

Arabians do well in endurance races even on the roughest types of land. The Tevis Cup race is a 100-mile (161-km) one-day trail ride that covers a rugged portion of the Sierra Nevada Mountains in Utah and California. Throughout the ride horses climb at least 15,000 feet (4,570 meters). Since the first Tevis Cup in 1955, all of the winners except two were partbred or purebred Arabians.

Physical Condition

Endurance racing horses must be in good physical condition. Endurance races have vet checks, or checkpoints. At each checkpoint veterinarians make sure each horse is fit to continue the race. They check the horse's pulse and breathing rate. They also make sure the horse's legs are not injured.

The first 10 horses that finish a race can compete in the best condition judging. Veterinarians consider the time of race completion and the horse's physical condition to decide on a winner. They also consider the amount of weight the horse carried.

Training

Training for endurance racing can take several years. Horses competing at national or international levels usually have at least three years of endurance training.

People training horses for endurance racing work their horses often. Many people ride their horses several times each week.

Beginning endurance riders start training by going on short rides. At first rides should be no longer than 3 miles (4.8 km). Horses can slowly work up to rides 15 to 25 miles (24 to 40 km) long.

Riders teach their horses to trot at a steady, fast pace. A steady, fast trot helps horses use more oxygen.

After three to nine months horses may be ready for more advanced training. Riders can start **cantering** more often. They also may start traveling over rough land or hills.

Napoleon Bonaparte's Arabians

Napoleon Bonaparte was emperor of the French empire from 1804 to 1814. He rode Arabians on his military campaigns. The remains of two of his favorite Arabian stallions can be seen today. The skeleton of Marengo is on display at the National Army Museum in London, England. Marengo is credited with saving Napoleon's life in battle. Taxidermists at France's Musée de l'Armée have restored the preserved body of Le Vizir, Napoleon's last horse.

canter—a gait of a horse that is faster than the trot and slower than the gallop

Chapter 4
Arabians in Action

People who train their horses for endurance riding can compete in many races. Most of these races are local or regional. Top riders compete at national and international levels. International races include the FEI World Equestrian Games and the European Endurance Championships.

Shows

Endurance racing is not the only talent of Arabians. Arabians are popular show horses. Some people show Arabians at open shows with other breeds. Other people compete at shows only for Arabians.

Arabian horse racing is popular around the world.

25

At shows events are divided into classes. People ride their horses in many classes. In halter classes handlers lead their horses by a halter. Horses are judged on their physical features and their ability to stand in a show position.

OTHER EVENTS

Crowds go wild when they watch Thoroughbreds speed around a track. Arabian racing is less popular, but it is still exciting. Each year the Arabian Racing Cup holds its Darley Awards. The awards recognize the best racehorses, jockeys, trainers, and others in Arabian racing.

Since 2003 the AHA has held its Sport Horse National Arabian and Half-Arabian Championship. Sport horses compete in jumping events and do advanced moves in **dressage**.

A pasture allows space for Arabians to run.

dressage—a riding style in which horses complete a pattern while doing advanced moves

It's Cooler in Texas

Summer is very hot in the country of Qatar. It's so hot that the royal family who owns Marwan Al Shaqab, a famous Arabian stallion, sends him to Texas to keep cool. Marwan stays at Michael Byatt Arabians in New Ulm, Texas. The stallion is a three-time World Champion and a two-time U.S. National Champion.

Marwan has sired many champions. People pay $20,000 for him to father babies. He has nearly 1,000 offspring around the world. Marwan is treated like a superstar in Qatar. In Texas he enjoys rolling in the mud and being treated like every other horse at Michael Byatt's farm.

Owning an Arabian

Owning a horse is a big responsibility. Like all horses, Arabians need a great deal of care. Owners must provide food, water, and shelter. Arabians also need large, open spaces to exercise.

Arabian owners often keep their horses at their farms or stables. Some owners pay to have their horses stay at another person's stable.

A Beloved Breed

Arabians are just as treasured today by their owners as they were by the Bedouins long ago. The classy appearance and talent of the world's oldest breed are sure to keep attracting new owners and riders.

Fast Facts:
The Arabian Horse

History: The Arabian horse breed began in the Arabian Peninsula in southwestern Asia. The Bedouins used them as war horses in the desert. In the 1800s people brought Arabians to Europe, North America, and other parts of the world.

Height: Arabians are 14.2 to 15.2 hands (about 5 feet or 1.5 meters) tall at the withers. Each hand equals 4 inches (10 centimeters).

Weight: 800 to 1,100 pounds (360 to 500 kilograms)

Colors: bay, gray, chestnut, black, roan

Features: dished head; large eyes; small, pointed ears; long, curved neck; small muzzle; short, straight back; high tail carriage

Personality: lively, intelligent, loyal

Abilities: Arabians are known for their endurance. They are able to carry heavy loads over long distances. Most top endurance racing horses are Arabians. Arabians also are good show and trail horses.

Life span: about 25 to 30 years

Glossary

ancestor (AN-sess-tur)—a member of a breed that lived a long time ago

breed (BREED)—a group of animals that have the same features and ancestry; breed also means to mate animals so they will produce young

canter (KAN-tur)—a gait of a horse that is faster than the trot and slower than the gallop

dressage (druh-SAHJ)—a riding style in which horses complete a pattern while doing advanced moves

endurance (en-DUR-enss)—the ability to keep doing an activity for long periods of time

mare (MAIR)—an adult female horse

registry (REH-juh-stree)—an organization that keeps track of the ancestry for horses of a certain breed

stallion (STAL-yuhn)—an adult male horse that can be used for breeding

withers (WITH-urs)—the top of a horse's shoulders

Read More

Kolpin, Molly. *Favorite Horses: Breeds Girls Love.* Crazy About Horses. North Mankato, Minn.: Capstone Press, 2015.

Osborne, Mary Pope, and Natalie Pope Boyce. *Horse Heroes.* Magic Tree House Fact Tracker. New York: Random House Books for Young Readers, 2013.

Young, Rae. *Drawing Arabians and Other Amazing Horses.* Drawing Horses. North Mankato, Minn.: Capstone Press, 2014.

Internet Sites

Use FactHound to find Internet sites related to this book.

Visit *www.facthound.com*

Just type in 9781543500318 and go!

Check out projects, games and lots more at *www.capstonekids.com*

Index

American Endurance Ride Conference (AERC), 18
Arabian Horse Association (AHA), 9, 26
Arabian Horse Club of America, 9
Arabian Racing Cup, 26

Bedouins, 4, 6, 7, 27
Blunt, Wilfred and Anne, 8
Bonaparte, Napoleon, 23

care, 27
Cass Olé, 15
chest, 14
colors, 10

Darley Awards, 26
Davenport, Homer, 8
dressage, 26

endurance racing, 18, 20, 21, 22, 24
European Endurance Championships, 24

FEI World Equestrian Games, 24
Grant, Ulysses S., 8
head, 12–13
jumping, 26
legs, 14
Marwan Al Shaqab, 27
Muhammad, 7
nostrils, 14
personality, 15
shows, 24, 26
size, 12
Tevis Cup, 21
track racing, 26
training, 22–23